SEXPULSION:

A Thrilling Erotic Story Between A
Priest And A Lady

Jorge Smith

Table Of Contents

Part 1: The Visit Of The Spirits

The renowned coffee company Sechxpresso was running a successful marketing that week at some of the Café spots in Italy. For every six cups of coffee someone consumed, the consumer would receive two cups of espresso with the Sechxpresso logo for free.

Katherine considered it a nice idea to drink some coffees at the neighborhood Café. The restaurant was packed, and she had to sit down at the bar. She ordered the first coffee, after two minutes the second one, after 4 minutes, the third one. Katherine was quite unquiet. In five minutes, she ordered five coffees.

The guy in black sat opposite her did not prevent himself from noticing and remarking about it with her.

- It appears you are quite keen to receive the two cups of coffee for free.

- Well, said Katherine, a little ashamed. It's not only that, the reason I am drinking so much coffee. I want to keep myself awake tonight.

- Why do you have any vital job to accomplish at night?

- No, I would love to sleep in fact, but .... Hey, there is something strange happening to me everytime I go to sleep and I am just frightened of it.

- Crazy? May I know what it is?

- No. No one would trust me anyhow.

- Ok. Let me tell you something that could benefit you. Every Thursday afternoon there is a priest in that modest chapel on the top of the hill, who listens to dozens of individuals with issues who need to confess something or just chat about some difficulty. Why don't you pass by there?

- "May I have one more coffee, please?" — requested Katherine to the waitress.

- "It's not healthy to drink so much coffee at once. Excuse me, but I must go. Think about going to church."

Katherine merely gazed at the guy without saying anything, like someone who was already thinking about what he offered.

The last faithful in the chapel was exiting the confessional when Katherine got there Thursday afternoon.

She walked in the little chamber, closed the curtain, peered quickly through the small holes at the wood wall which separated her to the priest to make sure he would be there to listen and, in a low and uncertain voice, she began to explain about her condition.

- "I was suggested to come here to discuss my situation. I don't know who could believe me and assist me."

- "I am here for that, to listen to you and try to assist. Tell me, what is your issue? "

- "I have been living alone for a few months in a rented flat here in the town. I don't have relatives or friends here and sometimes I feel lonely. But lots of times, I feel.... I feel..." — Katherine struggled to conclude the statement.

- "How do you feel? Tell me."

- "I felt aroused. Very horny. I began to pay more attention to men's bodies, envision heated sex and... I just started to touch myself very frequently."

- "I don't know what you call hot sex. Do you have a husband, a boyfriend, a partner with whom you could think of having sex with? If you have and love him, it's not a terrible problem to feel some of these emotions occasionally. But if you are alone, you should avoid these thoughts even to not provoke similar emotions in people who are committed to others."

- "I have no one. I must admit that lots of times I prefer to dress more provocatively. I have to say that the way I was, or I am, has never worried me. I confess, I was never a religious person. If I did not feel so terrified today, I would not be here."

- "Afraid?"

- "Yes, terrified. Something occurs constantly to me, that makes me question whether this is due the way I am".

- "And what is it?"

- "Some time ago, I simply could not help it, and I thought practically every day and night of sex even if I do not have a partner. I walked naked at home and spent lots of weekends afternoons playing with myself.

One night I was in my bed, I started to sleep, I woke up in the middle of the night, refused to open my eyes and I had the sensation that someone was there in the bed with me.

I could feel clearly that there was someone caressing my legs under the blanket. I did not understand how it could be possible; I knew I was alone in the apartment and the door was closed. It was weird, but somehow, I had no fear. I was enjoying it so much, I just kept my eyes closed and enjoyed the feelings.

I could feel that energy suddenly on the top of my body and its strange "light touching" then in the middle of my legs and suddenly I felt I was being penetrated. I've gotten totally wet and had the clear impression that a spirit was having sex with me.

My breath got faster, I got wetter, hornier but everything was still in a calm way. I did not move, simply felt and had a great pleasure.

After a while it stopped suddenly. I kept myself thinking of this experience and really wishing that it would happen again."

- "And did it happen again"?

- "As my spirit lover was taking too long to visit me, I decided to risk having sex with a man. I brought someone home, tried it, but it was not good.

I brought a second one, it was ok, but not good enough to bring him a second time. I was very much frustrated. I brought a third one, but he wanted to have a serious relationship and I did not want it, at least, not with him.

Then I stopped attracting guys to me and after some weeks I had again the feeling I was being visited by my spirit lover, but this time it was different.

The spirit was not so tender to me. Much on the opposite, I felt myself abused and I wanted to open my eyes and I could not. I had no control over my body, it was horrible.

He was hurting me, and I tried to say it, but I could not for some minutes, until I got totally desperate and my voice suddenly came out and I shouted, "get away". I was sweating, nervous and afraid.

I turned on the light, looked around my bedroom to see if I saw something different and tried to tell myself that there was nothing to be afraid of, so I went to the toilet. There I touched me, and I saw, I was bleeding in the middle of my legs. But it was not because of my period. I was not having it those days``.

- "Did you sense when you were awake, that you were actually raped"?

- "Yes...and when I saw the blood I was sure, I was. I felt afraid and had problems sleeping again. I had the impression that this time, it was not the same energy, spirit of the other time.

One week later it happened again and this time I heard for one second a male voice saying a word to me, which I could not understand.

I felt something scratching my ass, I got afraid and got totally awake. It took me a long time to sleep again that night. The next day when I was taking my shower and I looked in the mirror, I saw a scratch on my ass. I got goosebumps."

- "Oh my God! It looks severe".

- "I began to converse alone at home, with the certainty that one or all these ghosts would hear me. I inquired who he or they were. Why were they there?"

- "And did they answer"?

- "Not with words, but one time, asking that, the television turned on alone, out of nothing. I was far away from the remote control. I hardly watch TV. Other two nights, I was sleeping. I woke up in the middle of the night, because the TV turned on alone, again.

After a while without spiritual visits, I thought that things went calmer. I've gotten a telephone call from one of these guys that wanted a stable relationship with me, and he told me that after leaving my apartment when we met last time, he felt so badly that he had to go to the hospital immediately.

He stayed a couple of days there and the doctors did not find the reason that he got so bad, with pain in the stomach, nauseas, and high blood pressure. I thought it strange but did not give much importance until the next spiritual visit.

This same night, it happened again. I was in the dark, not yet sleeping completely and suddenly I could not move my body. I felt this aggressive energy on my body, touching me and squeezing me everywhere. I was almost in panic and I only could have control of my body again after some long minutes.

I did not leave the bed this time.. just thought about what happened. The next day, I noticed, I was full of bruises on my body".

- "What's your name"?

- "Katherine. Katherine Lyndth".

- "I am afraid you provoked, taunted, drew some of the terrible spirits with your overly feminine and sinful behavior, Katherine.

They know you; they see and observe you all the time. And they wish to use your body and punish you because they see the way you are.

Your seduction disturbs their peace and even if you do not want, your horniness holds them in this world. You must understand that you alone are the only one responsible for what's happening now.

And they can be bad not only with you, but with whoever comes closer to you, because some of these spirits can be jealous. Look what happened with this man who you had contact with. We must calm down these spirits and only once they are satisfied, they get what they expect from you and we can send them away".

- "I am afraid! I did not plan to tease any ghosts. I was never a person who goes frequently to the church, but I am Catholic. Do you believe me"?!

- "Yes, I do. The universe is full of mysteries. There are things still difficult to explain, which make us afraid of. But one thing is for sure. Energies are never destroyed, and we are all individual energies. Spirits are nothing more than energies. There are the good and the bad ones. And because we can't see them, we can't know where they are, what they think or want. They can easily play with our lives".

- "I want them to vanish, please help me! I am anxious to send them away. I don't know what to do. I am terrified of sleeping".

- "I will assist you Katherine, but again, you must accept that you are guilty to wake them up and attract them. You yourself confessed, you like to dress provocatively and tease men. You did not provoke only the living men, but also the dead ones". Katherine began to weep.

- "That's dreadful! I don't want to continue living with this pain. I never again will dress so seductive, I did not know...", the priest stopped her.

- "You did not know you could wake up the sexual wishes of the spirits, that's what you learnt now. Your behavior was obviously so abusive, with this change of men you told me, that the spirits started enjoying observing you. You are a slut, and you must recognize it. The spirits did already".

- "I know I was playing", said Katherine sobbing and tried to lessen her error.

- "You were much more than fun Katherine. You were and you are a horny decontrolled slut". Katherine sobbed copiously. – "There is only one way to send them away", concluded the priest with a strong voice. –

"There must be a sacrifice. Do you understand? They will only go away, when they see, that the one who aroused them, who evoked their souls by using means that men cannot resist, has pain, and is sexually used.

These spirits want now and deserve it, to see how much wet you get when you are used according to their wishes. They are keen to see, how fragile and impotent a slut like you gets when is used and tortured.

They will not give peace to you or any of the men that approach you while we do not give them what they are craving for. And we should act soon, otherwise, they could get more irritated or violent. You are the sacrifice they are waiting for".

- "I am the sacrifice"?

- "You are not yet, but you must be the sacrifice in one or more ceremonies".

- "Rituals"?!

- "Yes, we will probably need more than one ritual to satisfy and calm the bad spirits down. To deal with spirits, we need to make a special ceremony to evoke the presence of their souls. Only this way, we shall expect that they observe us and accept your sacrifice. You must understand the importance of these rituals and you must voluntarily offer yourself as the sacrifice".

- "I am terrified of it"!

- "I know you are afraid, it's completely normal. But as the chef of this chapel, a priest and someone who cares about all souls, someone who you know, you can trust and would never harm any one of my sheep, someone who is experienced and able to set contact to these spirits, I will guide this ceremony and can grant you, that although you will have to pass through some painful and embarrassing time, you will feel much better later. Even if you keep some temporary marks on your body.

I know what's good for you. You must remember, you are a sinner, and you deserve it indeed. This is what the spirits demand. To get you punished, humiliated.

And by sacrificing freely, yourself, you admit you are a sinner. This is what the bad spirits are awaiting. They know how dirty you can be.

They observe you all the time. And the dirtier they judge you are, the more and longer they will ask to see you being sacrificed. That means, maybe we need several days, months to satisfy the bad spirits".

- "Do you believe they will ask for that? To whom?"

- "To the one who will command the ceremonies. In our case, me. You can of course look for another priest to do that, but it must be a pure religious man and remember: the longer it takes to serve the wishes of the spirits, the worse your nights and days will be. I can feel your fear and the bad spirits surrounding you and they will let me know what they expect me to do with you".

- "Sounds terrifying! I don't believe I would be able to tell my secret a second time, to a second priest or anybody. I want to solve fast this issue and get back my serenity"

- "It might seem horrible, but consider that the situation can get worse and uncontrollable if we don't do something now".

- "I see and...I will sacrifice myself for the sake of my serenity".

- "..and the calm of these miserable souls you inspire", concluded the priest. Katherine gazed down feeling terribly desolated. – " Good! Knowing now what is happening and the seriousity of the subject, I could, as a priest, take you immediately as a sacrifice by forcing you and perform whatever it's necessary to please these souls. I myself don't want to have bad spirits around me or this town. As a priest, I must protect this place and my chapel. Bad spirits can become very dangerous. But it can also be that they don't accept me if I take you by force. Besides that, it would be more traumatic for you, if I would force you and.."

- "..no, no ...", interjected Katherine, - " I trust you priest and will give myself in your hands for this sacrifice. I would not dare, particularly after my recent experience, to question your holiness".

- "I am delighted you appreciate my wisdom and authority. Can we make an appointment for this Sunday? I have a mess here in the morning and afternoon, but you might come to the chapel at 17:00. I will arrange everything here and the altar for the ritual".

- "The altar here in the chapel"?!

- "Yes, of course, soon or later, we shall need the altar. It's vital".

- Ok, I will come Sunday at 17:00. I will depart immediately.

Katherine entered the place of confession at the same moment the priest opened his listener cabin and got a surprise. The priest was precisely the guy in black who was seated opposite her at the Café.

- "You!!! What's your name priest?" – inquired Katherine.

- "Arthur. Call me Priest Arthur, or just priest.

Part 2: The First Ritual

The sky was dark gray full of thick clouds that Sunday when Katherine arrived at the church utilizing a plain white blouse, a midi gray skirt and a shawl on the shoulders. She approached the chapel entrance, spotted priest Arthur kneeling on a pew seat next to the altar, praying and moved along the nave in his direction.

Gregorian music dominated the room. Katherine stopped alongside the priest. He looked serious at her, got up from the floor, grabbed her arm, walked her to a back chamber of the church and stated calmly:

- "Let us give the spirits the pleasure they require Katherine, so that they may go and leave you in peace.

A noisy dirty wood door allowed entry to the gloomy chamber. There were only two little and dusty windows in it.

The walls were covered by an old red and gold wallpaper. There was not much furniture there except a wood desk with a chair, a half-destroyed commode, a strange piece in the middle of the room, a cross and some pictures on the walls. There were wooden beams on the ceiling and two long black scarves were hung on them.

Several candles were set on the floor around the boundaries of the room. A tiny tablecloth covered part of the commode and on top of it, there were several glasses, a huge bottle of water, two bottles of wine, one already opened, a candlestick with three candles and a crop.

- "God will not object if we drink some blessed wine throughout the ceremony. It may enable us to relax. Would you want some? "

- "Yes, please".

Katherine grabbed her glass of wine and approached the drawings on the wall. They stimulated her a mix of sensations, between dread and arousement. The first image showed a nude lady in the midst of various monsters.

A priest was beside her with a glass in front of him. A horrible big dark animal with horns dressing a mantel was in front of this woman. They were all looking at her.

The second illustration also showed a naked woman on an altar. A priest beside her had her arms open and a sacred chalice on her belly. There were other naked women around, one of them seemed to beg something from heaven.

Two of these ladies looked to be nuns. A clothed lady on the left carried a high cross near to the woman on the altar as an apparently dead animal walked approaching her corpse.

On the right of the image, near a column the devil with a long tail and horns was penetrating from behind a clothed lady. There was a fog surrounding the area, and everyone looked to be in a trance.

Katherine glanced at the artwork for some minutes, took a long drink of wine and thought about the spirits that are visiting her. Priest Arthur studied her. She went inquisitive to the next one.

The scenery of the third picture was clearly inside of a church. There were some priests on the left and the right side, all of them wearing a dark hooded robe covering their heads. A huge, horrible animal with horns was penetrating a naked woman in the center. The priests did not show any movement giving the viewer the impression that they approved what was happening.

The illustration did not show the face of the woman, but just her lower body parts. Katherine got scared again, but also very much interested.

The final one portrayed a nude lady sleeping and several hideous little animals on her body.

- " This is a replica of a renowned artwork by Henry Fuseli, produced in 1781. The name of it is "The nightmare". Maybe you may recognise yourself in this case".

- "Do you suppose that the ghosts who are visiting me are hideous like that?

"

- "Much probable. The terrible spirits have never a pleasant look, since their images are the mirror of their awful souls.

Katherine got goosebumps and completed her wine glass. Arthur did not wait a second to fill it again.

- "These old illustrations Katherine show that since ever the church knows about the strong sexual wishes of bad spirits and how important it is to get rid of them. The one who attracts them must be punished for it. And satisfying the needs of these bad spirits we can get rid of them. You cannot escape from that. I can already now feel the presence of these spirits.

Priest Arthur closed his eyes and at this time a powerful thunder created a tremendous boom. Katherine felt afraid and as a reaction, grabbed both hands to her lips.

- "The spirits sent me a sign, Katherine. They want to have some of them punishing you and utilizing you. They expect that you acknowledge at first that you phoned them with your misbehavior. There is only one method to achieve it. I have a few masks for these tough occasions and by using one of them, while punishing you, the spirits will appreciate since they will perceive me as one of them. They will then grow quieter and will whisper in my ears, what I should do next.

A piece of sheet, a copybook, a pen, and a flashlight were put on the desk. Katherine was asked to sit on the chair and replicate what was written on the sheet.

- "While you drink your wine and create this copy, at least two times per line, I will obtain a mask which may be like one of these spirits that are about us.

- "No, please, don't leave me alone here!

"

- "It's merely for less than a minute my sweetheart. Don't worry! Nothing will happen with you now, while I am close to you and the spirits are desperate expecting to see you punished.

Priest Arthur left the room and Katherine took another sip of wine and another good look at the pictures before sitting and writing. Suddenly the wonder of what might be written on the paper was stronger than the fascination with the photos. She moved towards the desk, sat down and began reading. She felt ashamed, nonetheless made the replica.

The priest came back using a black medieval priest garb with a hood. Katherine quickly recognized herself in one of those photographs' scenarios. He asked her if she had done and she said she needed some more time. He positioned himself right in front of the desk eyeing her incredibly close. The entire environment altered Katherine' attitude, the heavy rain outside, the thunder, the loud Gregorian music, the darkness of the chamber, the candles everywhere, the thick voice of the priest, his medieval garb, and the terrible images.

- "I became a priest".

- "Then step up in the center of the room and read it out for the spirits. They will listen to you. I will put my mask on, and I want you to view me now not as the priest, but as one of these spirits who injured you in the night.

Priest Arthur donned a hideous rubber mask symbolizing a very nasty wicked guy. Katherine' heart began to beat faster. She started reading with a shaky voice.

- "I am a wicked lady and preserve the spirit of a huge slut.

I admit that I like walking around naked and think very often of sex, although I am not married.

I confess, I like touching myself and playing with my body until I get wet, and I reach an orgasm.

I admit, I appreciated the penetration of the first ghost that visited me.

I confess I had sex with several men, I attracted them, brought them home just to have sexual pleasure.

Although I did not intend to provoke you spirits, I am weak and can't control my sex drive.

Spirits, please accept my sacrifice as a form of repentance. I offer my body for punishment and humiliation".

- "Very excellent Katherine. Now take your scarf, your shoes, set them aside, remove your panty and present it to me", stated the priest with a peculiar voice due to the mask.

Katherine hesitated for a second but decided to comply.

– "Now bend over on this special pew bench Katherine". He pointed to that weird furniture in the middle of the room. It was a strange seat to kneel with a support for the stomach to lean down and a place for the elbows. Katherine opened the legs to be able to stand her knees on the leather. The priest helped her to understand which position she should take and pushed her back down so that the elbows could lean on the leather part of the front of the furniture. He took the crop from the top of the commode, came behind her and lifted her skirt letting her ass completely visible.

- "The spirits will beat you now Katherine, not me. They need it and you know, you deserve it. You will feel some discomfort, but it is important. I will attempt to moderate the urges of the spirits, so that you don't receive too much harm already in the first ceremony. They also demand that you return here again until you make them all pleased and display absolute remorse. If you cannot longer endure the agony or need a respite, you only respectfully ask the spirits to stop or give you some time. And remember! It's not the priest Arthur that will punish you today, but the ghosts".

The priest yelled out loud some things in Latin, which Katherine could not comprehend anything.

- "Haec femina peccatum non meretur poenas recipere et nunc. Ut vir Dei, quem pauperes non agnoscis spirituum sunt provocatus sum unicus, huius libidinis peccator. Nunc suscipe dignos paenitentiae et uti recte punire corpus meum in vobis. I will hit you first five times. You may count them in your thoughts and I will count as well".

The masked priest gave the first stroke on the right side of Katherine' ass and with pleasure heard her noise reaction. He moved his body to have the best position to hit her ass again, but this time on the left side of her ass. Without hurrying and very concentrated on what he was doing, as if he had to perfectly hit a golf ball towards a far small hole, he gave the third hit, this time again on her right side. For each stroke, Katherine made a loud "HAU!

". By completing the five strokes, he asked Katherine if she was alright. He offered her a drink of water, which she sipped still on the floor. She thanked him, handed him back the glasses and he brought the glass of wine.

- "Drink Katherine. The holy wine will assist you to endure the anguish you deserve".

Katherine agreed with him and took a nice drink.

- "Thanks".

- "I shall continue again with an additional five strokes. I can sense that the spirits are anxious to have more. Did we finish on the right side of your ass? Then I shall resume with the left now.

The priest kept beating Katherine' ass, right and left side alternately, with the same slow tempo and satisfaction. After concluding this second round, Katherine had the eyes still closed when he moved closer and stroked her ass. She felt an instant comfort and guilty for appreciating the hands of the priest on her ass.

- "The ghosts are speaking in my ears Katherine. They attempt to convey that they are really dissatisfied, since they cannot see marks on your ass. They need to see your body now married somehow and I will beat you three times on each side with my hands. Maybe this may quiet them.

Priest Arthur bent over his body to reach her ass with his hand. This time Katherine screamed much louder at each hand stroke he gave. The man was strong and determined to leave some marks on her. Katherine was almost crying after the third one and asked him to stop. He did stop for a minute and then continued with the left three, he said, he would give her. By finishing, he caressed her red ass. Katherine liked the caress and he liked the redness.

- Stand up! Remove all your clothing.

- "All my clothes?

"

- "You heard what I said"; he responded with a forceful voice.

- "Where should I place them?

"

- "Can you give them to me?

"

- "May I take a taste of wine before?

"

- "Yes, of course".

A bit shy, she removed the shirt first and gave it to him. The rain got stronger again. Katherine was slim and very feminine. Priest Arthur liked her figure and thought that the cotton bras could not give good support to her ugly, long, and flabby boobs. But he especially liked this type of breasts, they were very saggy. He took her shirt in his hands and waited for the next piece of cloth. When Katherine removed her bra, her breasts changed even more. They looked like two hanging sausages. By thinking how playful they were, his body gave a different shape to his priest robe. Katherine looked at his masked head and tried to guess what he was thinking of her. She was very embarrassed to pass him her bra and while giving it with one arm, she tried to hide her breasts with the other. He loved to notice her embarrassment.

- "Show now the spirits of the remainder of your body Katherine. It should not be too tough for you as you were regularly strolling nude at home".

- "Now, in front of you, it is very difficult".

- "The priest you met here serves just as a guide through this necessary ritual Katherine. My body now is lent, occupied by one of these spirits and he asks me to say to you, that he saw you several times naked and you should give me your skirt".

Katherine removed her skirt and gave it to him. She had a very hairy vagina although her legs were not. The priest got very aroused, took a thick red pen from a hidden pocket.

- "The spirit orders me to mark your body with words that he wants you to read later, when you are back home. Bend over on the desk and show me your ass".

Priest Arthur scribbled as large as he could: "This ass deserves many more marks and will receive it". Although she did not know what was written on her, she was loving the situation.

- "Now turn to me".

He drew big circles around the aureoles of her tits and wrote on them: "Sinner slut with floppy teats" – "The spirits will make sure your boobs will hang even more". He bent down his body to reach her abdomen and wrote: "Offer this hairy cunt for us sinners, or we will take it forcefully while you sleep". He wrote on her legs: "Bitch, dirty wet slut. You will get the fuck you were hoping for". The priest seized her head by pulling her hair to the back and wrote in bold letters on her forehead, "SINNER". He dropped the pen, twisted her nipples as she moaned and commanded her to say five times aloud: "I deserve the agony you give me SIR. I am a sinner". Then he started pulling down her pussy with one of his hands and almost shouted at her, ordering her to carry on repeating the same sentence, admitting that she deserves the pain. While she suffered and nervously repeated it, he also recited something aloud in Latin. Katherine had a mix of physical pain and weird pleasure, started to get confused and slightly wet between her legs. Coincidentally a lightning bolt cleared the sky and the room for a second and the thunderclap convinced Katherine that it was the spirits manifesting.

He noticed that she was more relaxed and finally gave in to the ritual.

- "You sinful slut, lay down on this desk, raise your legs and spread them widely".

Without contesting she did as she was asked. The masked priest touched her cunt with his finger to make sure she was wet enough, and she moaned. He lifted his long cloth and pushed slowly his long hard cock into her cunt while saying something in Latin. She looked at him, as if she would believe that there was really a horrible creature penetrating her. She looked around the candles, the strange furniture, the bad weather through the window, listened to the sound of that scary Gregorian music, the thunder, the hooded priest with that horrendous mask, closed her eyes and decided to let it go. Both, sinner, and sinner had a terrific orgasm.

Priest Arthur laid down his towel, assisted her to leave the desk without a word, handed her another glass of wine, poured him a drink as well and eventually took the mask from his head. He was sweating and his hair was utterly disheveled.

- "The spirits are quiet now, Katherine. I am delighted that you cooperated and served them. But they will not disappear so easily. You will have to come back shortly for a future session.

- "I understand, priest", replied Katherine with her head down, but deeply pleased.

- "Let us schedule another appointment to hear what the spirits are waiting for from you. Can you come in one week? Next Sunday at the same time?"

- "I suppose so".

- "Good! Before sleeping, don't forget to pray and to thank that you are properly guarded by me, a loyal servant of God.

- "I will, Sir. Do you suppose they will let me sleep tonight? "

- "I am sure they will! During the week, pay attention to the signs. It might be that they observe you. But if you obey all my directions, they will vanish".

They completed the wine glasses and the rain eased down.

- "The weather got better now. You are fortunate Katherine. Or this is a sign from the sky that you performed well and it's time to go home. You may take your clothing back and go now. I will meet you in one week".

- "Good night priest!

"

- "Good night Katherine".

Part 3: The Third Encounter

Katherine drove back feeling a combination of remorse and delight. Arriving home, she searched quickly for the large mirror, anticipating to read what was written on her body before she removed all of it under the shower.

She was surprised to realize how unclean, sloppy she appeared. It took several minutes before she could read the writing and once again, she felt very ashamed. She bathed for a long time and had trouble completely erasing the writing.

While bathing, she thought whether she was truly a sinner or simply a victim of wicked or lustful spirits. She was undoubtedly a sinner, since she could not deny herself that she was really aroused throughout the priest ceremony, so much so that she attained a wonderful orgasm. Maybe she was also possessed by a malevolent ghost, concluded her.

The following day the weather was excellent and sunny, but Katherine had to wear pants and a blouse with long sleeves to go to work, to properly conceal the remainder of the writing on her body that she could not get rid of. Despite that, she was in excellent humor. From time to time, she did a quiet retrospective of the preceding evening.

On Wednesday at noon Katherine went to eat something and have a coffee at the same Café, she loved to go from time to time.

She sat down at a table, the waiter handed a table set paper in front of her and inquired what she would like to have. She asked for a coffee and a small sandwich.

Everything looked to be as normal, if it were not for the advertising on the paper attracting attention for the tennis tournament and had a major name to announce, an Italian tennis player named Jannik Sinner. And the term Sinner was put in enormous type letters.

Katherine felt it unusual and pondered whether it was merely a coincidence or a hint from the spirits reminding her, what she is. That was the word most inscribed on her complete body.

The week appeared to pass slowly. Whatever wind Katherine sensed she imagined it may be a spirit nearby.

She felt lonely again Friday evening. So much, that she did not mind wondering that maybe a benevolent spirit may be viewing her.

She thought again about the priest, the ceremony and felt eager to recall that soon it would be Sunday, the day she would go for her second rite.

Katherine entered promptly at the church. She was bashful, a little apprehensive and really interested to undergo a next rite. Priest Arthur was waiting, again seated extremely in front. He donned black slacks with a belt and black shirt with the ordinary priest collar.

- "Good evening priest".

- "Good evening Katherine. Let's proceed to the ritual chamber".

They moved away to the punishment chamber without altering any word. The weird furniture in the center of the room was not there anymore and there was a bible on the desk this time.

The rest was the same. And again, there were two full Italian wine bottles on the commode. Arthur handed them the wine, the water and applauded with Katherine.

- "Let's cheer for the high moods and a successful session tonight".

- "Cheers!"

- "How did you spend the week? Any surprises?"

- "It was a peaceful week. Nothing spectacular.... except that.."

- "That what?"

- Something funny occurred at the Café we met. On the paper the waiter put in front of me, there was an advertisement for a tennis competition and its key tennis player is named Jannik Sinner. Sinner was the term you inscribed on my body. His surname was written in exaggerated size".

- "I see. But it was not precisely me who scribbled the word, but one of the spirits. They have numerous methods to provoke".

- "Do you believe that was a provocation?

"

- "Very certainly. Now sit down at the desk and duplicate what is written on the sheet. You may take your wine with you.".

- "Are you going to fetch a mask?

"

- "I will but will not put it on immediately. The spirits want me to see carefully what I do initially with you".

Katherine sat at the table, took the page in her hand, and began to read it. Arthur sipped his wine calmly and looked at her. She glanced at him and he spoke seriously.

- "Go on! Write it down and don't pay attention now to me."

Katherine glanced down, got the pen, and began copying the phrases to the notepad. Arthur left the room and came back with a blanket and a huge filled plastic bag.

He laid the blanket on the floor in the center of the room and the bag next to the commode. He kept sipping his wine and when he observed that Katherine had done her job, he requested her to remove all her clothing, knee on the blanket and read out loud what she wrote. Katherine started:

– "1 - I am a wicked woman, easy to be stolen by any male, so I deserve to be punished.

2 - I believe that Priest Arthur will assist me to detect my poor behavior and will punish me correctly ".

3 – The ghosts deserve to witness my nude body suffering and receiving marks.

4 – I admit, I am a sinner and must be bitten by the good priest.

5 – The ghosts will torment my body via the hands of the pious priest.

6 – I will stand resigned to my pain.

7 - I am willing to allow my body to be used by whatever the spirits decide tonight till they have their pleasure and release my consciousness. I realize that this is the only way to reclaim tranquility ".

- "That's it Katherine, this is the only way you may have serenity again. You must suffer now in front and for all spirits who are watching you with great sexual cravings.

Will you obey my demands, Katherine? Remember, it's not ME who will punish you now, but the spirits via my hands".

- "Yes, I will", responded Katherine displaying some dread in her voice.

- "Before we start with the rite, take a drink of wine to enable you to relax", said the priest offering her the glass. - "Drink some water too, Katherine. Otherwise, you could become intoxicated too fast".

From behind, Arthur put his left hand on her left shoulder and with the right one, started to slowly caress her back and butt. Katherine closed her eyes and enjoyed it. He approached in front of her and passed the hands on her breasts from up to down till his fingers reached her nipples. They became immediately hard.

- "They murmur in my ears, that while you have two ugly droopy sausages here, they are great to play with".

Katherine was deeply humiliated by hearing it and instantly sought to cover them with the arms.

- "No, do not conceal them", murmured the priest, pulling her arms aside . - "They want to study you all via my eyes and want you to know through my tongue, what they all think of you. They are various spirits Katherine and they all view you now and remark about you. You are the focus of attention for them now".

- "Don't they like my body? Are they laughing? "

The priest kneed in front of her, continuing to caress Katherine' breasts, closed the eyes, elevated his head, and inhaled deeply before replying.

- "Some of them, yes, they laugh and gossip about your hanging breasts. Others are serious and ordering me to pull hard on your nipples. They want to see them hard and to find out how long they can get.

Katherine complained with the sudden pulling of her nipples.

- "You may complain about Katherine, they enjoy it a lot. Now stand up and spread your legs ".

Katherine did it, although she was totally embarrassed. The priest took the bible from the desk, opened it, walked around Katherine saying something loud in Latin and placed the Bible back on the desk. Katherine wondered, what could those words mean.

- "Haec femina peccatum non meretur poenas recipere et nunc. Ut vir Dei, quem pauperes non agnoscis spirituum sunt provocatus sum unicus, huius libidinis peccator. Nunc suscipe dignos paenitentiae et uti recte punire corpus meum in vobis."

He kneed again on the floor close and in front of her, murmured again some Latin phrases, and pushed his nose in the center of Katherine pubic hairs.

- "They appreciate your aroma and your vagina hairs a lot. They want to have some of them. They told me several days ago. Therefore, I prepared the holy glasses earlier which would preserve them. We will need to clip some of your vulva hairs later".

The priest rose up, grabbed the long black ribbons which dangled from a wood beam, requested Katherine to open the arms apart and tied them up. He moved behind her, massaged her legs fully from behind, climbed up to her butts, and spoke in her ears.

- "I shall start Katherine. The spirits are glad to see you hurting. Count till five, like the other day. I shall create a pause then and will give you another five strokes ".

The priest took his belt and proceeded to beat Katherine' ass. The first hit on the right side, the second on the left, the third on the right again and so on.

For each time the belt struck her ass, the priest could hear Katherine screaming. After 10 strokes, he came in front of her and showed her two enormous nipple suckers, one hooked to the other with a long metal chain.

- "Do you know what those things are Katherine? They are nipple suckers. As the name says, they are made to suck. These suckers have a screw here, do you see Katherine? When I hold it around your areola and turn the screw, the formed vacuum inside will pull out your whole areola and nipple. It might be painful for you, but it's harmless in the end, and necessary. The spirits ask me to do that ".

Katherine expressed dread again on his face. He wrapped the first sucker around her left areola, twisted the screw slowly just a little and she instantly screamed. Her nipple grew noticeable.

He repeated the surgery on the right breast and returned to the left sucker to snug a little more the screw. Again, he screwed more than the sucker on the right side.

Katherine yelled with anguish. He continued thrusting the suckers till he saw she could not stand more. The plastic suckers dangling, giving the appearance, her drooping teats were much longer. Arthur could see her swelling areolas and nipples through the translucent plastic suckers.

- "Wonderful Katherine. Your nipples are enormous, extremely swollen and the spirits are appreciative that you suffer this discomfort for them".

- "This hurts a lot! ", exclaimed Katherine, practically weeping.

- "I know, but you are doing very well. You cannot disappoint the spirits, Katherine. Remember, you are the sacrifice. I am confident, you can and will suffer more to gain the peace from the spirits. You want to recover from your nice night of sleeping, no? ".

- "Yes, I do. ", she answered with a shaking voice.

- "Good! Imagine now this room full of miserable horny spirits, who you torment regularly for a long time. I can feel them all here about us. They adore seeing you like that, and they are giving me the orders of what to do ".

At this point, priest Arthur presented till her lips her glass of water. She took a drink.

- "Drink more Katherine. Drink the full glass. You must drink to replace the water you would lose with your tears ".

Katherine had in reality a tear on her cheek at this minute when he mentioned that. She sipped the full glass of water. He put the glass back on the commode, filled it promptly again and brought her glass of wine near to her lips.

- "Drink! The wine will enable you to endure the agony ".

She took many swallows of the wine, till she nearly emptied the glass. Arthur brought back her wine glass when she did not want anymore and swiftly finished it.

The priest grabbed a black wood crucifix with a hook from his satchel. He came in front of Katherine standing it, yelled out some Latin words, touched her forehead with the cross, while praying in Latin, touched her cunt with the cross and hung the cross on the chain that attached one breast to the other. Katherine yelled loudly jointly with his loud prayer.

- "The spirits want your sagging breasts to grow more saggier. Your teats bow down deliciously more now ".

Katherine had watery eyes, but restrained herself, to not weep. She bowed her entire upper body forward till the limit as her arms were fixed.

- "They think your sagging sausages now look like two pendulums and it suits this church ".

The priest screwed further both suckers connected to her breasts, pulled a whip out of his bag, stepped behind Katherine and said:

- "Count! This will provide tremendous delight for the spirits ".

Katherine was defeated again 10 more times. Whenever she was smacked, the cross swung and tugged her breasts to various directions. Katherine yelled and began to weep.

The priest moved closer to her from behind, stroked her breasts softly and asked her to speak out loud for the spirits: "Forgive me to be an uncontrolled slut ". Katherine repeated it nervously and with a voice ton of surrender.

- "Loud Katherine. Confess to the spirits what you are. They all want to listen to it from you ".

- "Forgive me to be an unrestrained slut ".

Somehow Katherine felt nice to say it loud. The forced confession along with the whip tempted her feminine impulses.

- "Now repeat out loud: 'Forgive me to love being penetrated by everyone '".

- "Forgive me to love getting fucked by everyone ".

The priest stepped in front of her, gave a flick on the crucifix to watch her response. She groaned again, uttering a loud "NO".

He brought the wine to her again, which she consumed cheerfully. Then he brought the water, but she drank only a sip, till he stressed to her that she should drink more.

She drinks half a glass. He filled both glasses, took himself a nice gulp of wine, pulled a paddle out of his luggage and told her to open her legs wider again.

The priest laid the paddle on the floor behind her, pulled the cross from the chain, walked behind her again, sat down on the floor with his head in the midst of her legs and said:

- "The spirits want to experience the flavor of your cunt via my tongue". The priest licked her vigorously till he felt that she had yielded to her sexual impulses irrespective of the discomfort.

Katherine loved it and sighed, shutting her eyes. The minute after he listened to her nose, he got the paddle and without witnessing his action, he whacked one of her ass sides.

She was astonished. He licked her again and after half a minute, he paddled the opposite side of her ass. She yelled. He swallowed her pussy large jumps for an occasion and spanked her again on one and the other side.

Katherine yelled out loud. Arthur quit his post to declare that they should relocate location. It was time to go to the altar. Katherine stated, she could not go. She had to urgently go to the toilet. The priest came again in front of her, closed his eyes and said:

- "What do you want to do on the toilet? Do you need to pee?"

- "Yes. ", responded Katherine ashamed.

- "The spirits allow you to pee Katherine, but they want to witness it and to have your pee preserved in a glass. You are not permitted to use any bathroom. They know I have several glasses with me".

By stating so, priest Arthur withdrew from his bag a not so tiny, not so large glass with lid. He severely removed the cover of the glass.

- "They say, I must lay this glass on the floor, and you may offer all your urine to them, pissing within it. If you pee outside and dirty the chapel floor, you get an additional ten strokes".

- "How can I pee within this little glass? It's impossible".

- "It's better for you to attempt, than to pee on the altar. There, the penalty would be much harsher".

- "I can't...it's...so it's embarrassing".

- "Indeed, but we will defy the spirits commands Katherine. They require it, to humiliate you. They want me to store your pee for them in the glass. Do your best. Relax and orient your crack to this glass".

Katherine could not restrain herself longer and followed his orders. Immediately as she began to discharge her bladder, she peed too forcefully and in front of the glass.

She shifted her body the way she could, to attempt to reach the inside of the glass. She felt horribly embarrassed, but terrified of being chastised again, she attempted to focus on her duties.

She could put a portion of the liquid into the glass, but most of it wetted the floor. At a certain point, she needed urgently to release herself and let everything go. The priest displayed his disgust by finding the chapel floor unclean.

- "You are such a pig! Look at the filth you did everywhere. We can scarcely walk around here now. You dirtied the holy chapel, you pig sinner. The spirits are also upset because you did not perform properly, and they urge me to punish you for that.

Priest Arthur removed a rubber pig snout with an elastic affixed to it from his backpack.

- "You are a really filthy pig Katherine. This nose matches wonderfully to you today and you deserve it. The spirits are delighted to see that I shall punish again the pig". The priest pulled a wooden stick from behind the commode and showed her.

- "This time you will feel the cane on your ass". He placed the pig nose on her. - "Now you can show all the spirits that you are truly a pig slut. Count Katherine".

Katherine counted again, this time weeping of a combination of agony and embarrassment.

- "Excuse yourself for dirtying the church floor Katherine!

", said the priest while stroking her.

- "I apologize for dirtying the church floor".

- "Again Katherine".

- "I apologize for dirtying the church floor".

- "Repeat to the spirits that you are a disgusting pig slut".

- "I am...I am a nasty pig slut".

- "Good. Say out loud to them, that the next time, you will do better. You will pee where they want and the manner they want".

- "Next time, I will do better. I will pee where they want and the manner they want".

After 10 strokes and plenty of cries Arthur stopped and inspected the ass of Katherine. It was red, full of markings, and it appeared that part of her blood would burst out of some of these marks at any moment. He massaged her ass and said:

- "Good Katherine. Your ass will be bloated for a long time. This is what the spirits need to see. Let's check whether your nipples are beautifully swelled as well".

By withdrawing the suckers Katherine cried again.

- "Look how long areolas and nipples you have now, Katherine! Amazingly large. They are as swollen as your ass. You look like an animal now. Your drooping teats appear so weary, so much heavier.

Wonderful outcome! The spirits are looking very near to your swelling nipples. I feel their presence right here. Now we should proceed to the altar. Keep the nose until I let you remove it".

Arthur untied her arms from the ribbons, and they moved towards the altar. He grabbed the blanket from the floor, his bag, and the bottle of wine with him. He laid the blanket on the altar and commanded her to lay down there.

There was a small ladder to help her to climb the altar. He took a body pen from his bag, started to say some Latin words out loud, and made a big cross between her breasts. Arthur ordered Katherine to lift her legs and hold them with the help of her arms. He took two pieces of rope and tied her wrists to her legs.

Katherine could not move much anymore. By constantly saying his Latin prayer, he took a long and thin red candle from his bag, he licked her cunt and slowly stuck the candle into her vagina.

Katherine moaned. He lit the candle and took a special big and thick metal glass, explaining to her that it was the sacred chalice.

He filled the chalice with some wine and put it on her tummy, holding it. He did some praying, touched the liquid with his fingers and allowed some drops to fall on each one of her nipples. He touched the wine again with his fingers and let some drops fall on her clitoris.

- "This hypothetical triangle I created now on you, uniting your clitoris with your nipples and placing your uterus in the midst of this assumed triangle, is a sign of connection between your feminine body and the good spirits, who are also observing you".

The priest kissed and licked softly a nipple, kissed and licked the other, kissed and licked her clitoris, raised the glass with the two hands, murmured some Latin words again and drank the remainder of the wine from the cup.

- "It is time to trim some of your pubic hairs to please the spirits".

Arthur got a little scissor and still with the lighted candle in her pussy, pulled part of her vulva bush with the fingers and chopped some of the hairs.

He put them inside a tiny glass, closed it and wrote on the glass in red with huge letters, "SINNER Katherine' CUNT HAIR". He repeated the process by cutting another quantity of her bush, put it in another little glass, closed it and wrote the same thing, "SINNER Katherine' CUNT HAIR".

- "One of these glasses the spirits will take with them Katherine. They ask me to have permanently something of you with them.

The other glass with your cunt bush will be placed here in front of the altar for the public. They want everyone to know that you are a confessing slut and you have to go through a ritual".

- "No, please priest! You cannot leave this glass with my name on it here in the church for the public! My reputation, my life here would be shattered".

- "It's not me who wants that Katherine. The spirits ask so. They want to see you humiliated. I can later pray extra, and attempt to persuade them to abandon this duty, but now they are all shouting here in my ears, 'no, no, no, we want it. The glass should be seen to the entire town'".

- "No, please.."

- "Let's go on with the ceremony and attempt to appease the spirits in the best manner".

Arthur withdrew the candle from Katherine cunt and drew on her ass two little crosses with the wax drips coming out of the candle, while praying loud. She shouted, horrified.

- "SPIRITS! Say to me now, what can I do more with this sinner, so that she pays the price for taunting all of you. Tell me! How can this harlot serve you better now?", yelled the priest gazing up to the roof of the church and with extended arms. Katherine was a little frightened. She did not want to be beaten anymore.

- "Yes, I hear you! I hear you ghosts... continue..."

- "What do they say?", said Katherine, seeking to disrupt his conversation with the beyond.

- "Yes, I see", the priest kept talking and staring above, dismissing the intriguing subject of his sacrifice. - "I understand.

Yes, we all know she is a sinner and must serve you all, but she acknowledged her guilt and accepted that she has no control over her sexual instincts. Please, select one of you, just one to use her now".

- "To utilize me?"

- "Yes, Katherine, I am pleading them, that only one of them is selected to use you now via my body and you should be glad if they accept my request, otherwise, all of them here would fuck you right now".

- "All of them? No...I cannot tolerate one more unpleasant event".

- "That's it...wait...wait...they are saying something to me". The priest closed his eyes, demonstrating tremendous focus and started out loud. - "I see. One of you was picked to make use of the sacrifice. I thank you for accepting my proposition."

- "What did they say"?

- "They accepted that only one will use you now and they decided who it should be. I will put on my mask now, according to what they decided about Katherine. Close your eyes until a second order".

Katherine closed her eyes. The priest went to his bag and removed a demon mask out of it. He positioned the short ladder that was near the altar, in front of Katherine exposed ass, put his trousers down, the mask on his head and raped her cunt.

She sighed a little and disobediently opened her eyes. When she saw the form of the devil screwing her, she screamed and thought of the painting at the church's particular chamber wall. From the mask emerged a weird heavy voice: - "You are not only a nasty pig slut Katherine, but also disobedient.

The priest advised, you should not open your eyes. Now you see, who my kids decided to watch using you. And they were correct when they gossiped to me, that you have a nice cunt. My cock likes it".

Despite the dreadful terrifying surroundings, Katherine began to become wet. She closed her eyes again and in a short time achieved a powerful orgasm. She felt dreadful, puzzled and partially horrified to have the thought that it may actually happen, that she allowed herself to enjoy pleasure by being exploited by the devil.

- "I will release my cum now within you slut", by concluding the statement, the masked priest also attained his climax. Sinner and sinner looked to be totally happy with the entire rite. The priest removed the mask and Katherine was happy to see the face of the priest again.

- "The spirits are extremely delighted", stated the priest with a hurried voice. - "For some time, they will not trouble you for sure. But simply for security, I must put something on you...to prevent that they assault you at night and that you misbehave".

- "To put what?"

The priest pulled a sanitary moist towel and a chastity band from his suitcase. He carefully cleansed her genital regions moving the towels from up downwards till all the come and perspiration gone.

- "What should you put on me?", inquired again Katherine frightened.

- "You will need to wear a chastity belt until I release you. This is for your own protection".

- "A chastity belt?! How will I be able to go to the toilet?!", said Katherine, frightened.

- "Don't worry. There is a hole on it made exactly that, women can still pee, and your ass will be completely free, so that you will be able to shit without problems. You will just not be able to be fucked next time, neither by a man, nor by any spirits, until we meet again. You can sleep in peace tonight".

Priest Arthur freed her arms and legs and assisted her to leave the altar. Once she was upright, he removed her pig nose and gently placed the chastity belt on her.

- "Do you see Katherine? These new chastity belts are not that unpleasant. This one is primarily leather. Just the chains behind and the locker on your waist are made of steel. At the front bottom you have this tiny hole, to enable that your urine goes through.

A penis cannot pass there. Therefore, even if you have your slut impulses, you won't be able to provide your cunt. The remainder of your pussy is covered by the leather, so that you can also not touch it. I agree that it will be a little tough to clean yourself and wash your hairy cunt.

You could grow a little stinky after some days, but since no guy can use you, this will not be a huge issue, till I unlock your belt again. These two chains might compress your butt-cheeks, but you can still sit and crap between them.

You will need to learn to sit straight upwards and you might feel some discomfort eating, I agree. You cannot exaggerate with the food. As I feel pity for you, I will not tidy it too much by locking it now. I recommend you dry it well with a hairdryer after shower, so that you avoid your pussy itching.

Mind also the material you choose. If you wear tight pants, people will wonder to themselves, what do you store there in the middle of your legs. It would surely be quite humiliating for you to explain.

You could opt to wear skirts next time. The benefit of the belt is that you don't need to use underpants.

- "How can I get a job like this?

".

- "The same route you always went! With your legs. You could walk and sit a little funny occasionally, but you must pay attention to your actions, so that the others do not notice anything.

This will be good to remember you continually that you teased the spirits with your body and now you deserve it.

You should ponder your dirtiness anytime you are alone". By saying so, Arthur locked the belt on her and pulled the key.

- "Will you trust me and give me the key"?

- "Of course not! The key will be secure with me. I determine when I should open it. You should believe me; I will not lose the key.

You may dress now. It's getting late. I am pleased with you, because you went so successfully through this process. I shall pray for your soul in the coming days".

- "Thank you, Father, but...and the glass?

", inquired Katherine pointing to the closed glass with her pubic hairs in it.

- "As I said, one glass, the spirits will take with them. The other must wait here, just in front of the altar. The spirits wish so".

Katherine did not like the notion but chose not to push at that moment. She was exhausted and wanted to inspect her marks alone, at home. She clothed herself and departed feeling very much puzzled with all that experience she had just experienced.

- "And when do we meet again, so that you may liberate me from the belt"?

- "What about next Sunday again? At the same time"?

- "I accept Sir. Next Sunday at the same time, despite it appearing to take a long time to have this belt on".

- "Don't complain Katherine! Be pleased to have all the spirits now satiated. I want you to go home now, relax, have a wonderful night of sleep and reflect well on the next few days, how excellent you did in sacrificing yourself for the will of these miserable individuals.

And remember, that if you do not act appropriately and respect my directions, they could grow much more demanding".

- "I won't be able to forget this evening for sure. Good night priest".

- "Good night, Katherine. Sleep comfortably and in peace".

Part 4: The Surprise

It was not easy to sleep with that chastity belt. Katherine left the bed early morning and while urinating, she saw her pubic hairs on the sides of the leather belt.

The entire past evening passed her head. She felt suddenly horribly embarrassed of all she was exposed to. She thought she should get more sanitary wet towels to clean her pussy better.

The belt did not make her life particularly practical. She regarded herself nude in the mirror and felt dominated and embarrassed again.

She turned to check her ass and noticed her buttocks were full with markings and bruises. She never dreamed; she could bear so much physical discomfort.

Katherine' thoughts were still focused on the prior evening, and she was moving and doing activities without attention.

She seized a shirt and a pair of pants to dress and while leaning down with some effort to dress the trousers, she realized, she should better wear a skirt. She went back to her closet and grabbed a longer skirt instead.

On the way to the job, she observed, she could not walk the same manner, calm and with the same pace. That Monday she was quieter and analyzed every move she made, to avoid notice.

By acting thus, it appeared, she drew even more glances to her direction. It was a terrible day for her, and she counted the hours to get back home. On the way back, she went by the local market and purchased the hygiene towels.

Somehow the concept of believing that the priest was holding the key to that intimate apparatus got her excited. "Could it be that I am feeling drawn to this guy, who battered and exploited me so much? It was not him!

The terrible spirits battered and humiliated me that way. He is only providing a conduit between me and these ghosts.

He a priest anyway and I should not allow myself to have sexual feelings for a guy from the church", concluded Katherine in her thoughts. She felt absolutely insane and bewildered.

The evenings used to be always a delight for Katherine, when she could sit down alone in her kitchen, savor with time a fine supper and contemplate about the day.

She had indeed joy at these moments, but that Monday it was not the same. As soon as she wanted to eat a little more, she felt she could not due to the belt.

It was crushing her tummy too much to relax her upper body and consume as much as she desired. She was really upset with that feeling and could do nothing, save laying down to relax the muscles.

"Women who desire to lose weight might use a chastity belt as a diet equipment aid. They would undoubtedly triumph", grinned her with her idea.

It was hard to get through Tuesday. Katherine was conscious, she must not lose concentration on her task. She was new in that firm, new in the area and had already signed a long-term rental deal to acquire her flat.

The town had not many habitants and if she screwed up her job there, it would not be simple to move to another excellent spot near to her new house.

She had consequently to focus on her profession, but since those ghosts came, her life seemed to take a peculiar turn. She did not know any more whether she missed the visit of the first ghost or the meetings with the priest.

She felt herself genuinely a sinner. In the evening, returning home, she was really hungry, but she thought about the awful sensation she had the night before and attempted this time to eat slowly and smaller portions.

It was not easy, and she felt not entirely fulfilled. Katherine had her shower, dried carefully the hairs, the belt and as much as she could of her pubic hairs.

She switched on the TV, flipped the stations and stopped in one of these Italians nonsense shows full of lovely ladies.

She pondered about what the spirits said about her, that her breasts are unattractive and drooping. She felt guilty by hearing it so plainly.

Katherine opened her night chemise and studied her breasts. Although they were far from being like those gorgeous Italian women's breasts, she always admired them.

Then she got another memory flash by recalling that the spirits added that while her breasts were unsightly, they were ideal to play with.

She grinned alone and became aroused by that. Katherine recalled her great urge to pee and how terrible it was for her to attempt to urinate within the glass.

- "Oh my God!", muttered her loud to herself, - "How could I pee in front of the priest and that manner! What does he think of me? But I could not hold it anymore. And the pig nose?!?!?!", humbled her.

The series of recollections from the prior Sunday made Katherine feel humiliated, nevertheless aroused again. She turned the volume of the television down as if it offended her reflection and began to play with her breasts.

Her nipples became erect, and she relished the notion that the ghosts may well be watching her. She felt she could simply not ignore her horniness and slid down with her hand to her pussy. She closed her eyes and loved sliding the fingers on her long pubic hairs.

She felt the weirdness of the chastity belt and thought that the priest may be all the while staring at its key and thinking about her. She felt like a sinner again, a wild horny sinner who was once again submitting to her sexual instincts.

She decided that the priest was accurate in everything he said about her. She attempted to obtain some pleasure by inserting a finger between the belt and her pussy, but it was difficult. She opened the eyelids and experienced a second of wrath by seeing her pussy trapped.

Katherine chose to detour her thoughts and headed to the kitchen again. Maybe the time elapsed was enough to risk a second round of meals. She prepared her modest lunch, sat down at the table and loved it.

Not yet free of her eager thoughts, as soon as she finished eating, she touched her belt again and toyed with her escaping bush.

- "My hairs are very long; should I clip them? Oh my God! Now I recall, he clipped my hair! And put them in a glass there, at the altar for everyone in this town see see! I suppose I drank too much last Sunday.

I had nearly forgotten about it", said Katherine alone, extremely frightened. - "I must take this glass from the church. Imagine if someone renowned goes there and finds my name there with my hairs and that sentence!

My God...and my name is totally, not a popular name! There are certainly not two Katherine in this crazy little town! I must go there, but now it is dark and too late and tomorrow I must work.

And moreover...priest Arthur cannot see me taking the glass from there. I must accomplish it secretly.", calculated Katherine, still in a loud voice. - "The chapel should be open and priest Arthur must be engaged with something or someone else, so that he does not witness me coming there and taking away that glass.

What a shame if someone sees it! No...no...I can't fathom that folks go to church in the middle of the week.

Everyone must work, and the church is constantly empty. I will attempt to obtain this glass tomorrow, after the job".

Katherine departed to the bed anxious, visualizing some of her few recently done colleagues during a mess in the chapel and getting near to the glass to verify what was written on it. It was tough to relax that night and sleep.

By leaving the job on Wednesday Katherine drove directly to the church. As she could not see any automobile nearby, she thought that the church was probably vacant.

She hoped the chapel was open and with some fortunate, she would not encounter the priest. Katherine quietly pushed the front door frightened of the notice of the priest, in case he was present, and the chapel was opened.

She took a careful glance before entering, did not notice anybody around and risked heading towards the altar without making noise. She was scared of seeing the priest there. She would not know how to justify her being there.

Fortunately, she reached the glass with her name. It was still there, just in front of the altar. Just one of the glasses. She grabbed it and rushed up to exit the church, still paying heed to not make noise.

She got swiftly in the vehicle and went right away, without glancing too much behind. Katherine felt immensely satisfied by having removed the proof of her misbehavior with her intimate hairs from the chapel. She felt protected again and could even smile.

The following day, Katherine was in better humor and attempted even better to accept her new imprisoned state. She was feeling so great that she felt, she may chance one of the regularly offers done by her coworkers to have lunch together.

Katherine and Eugênia went together for a brief lunch at a little restaurant near to the company where they worked. After making the order, they sought to find out more about each other.

- "Are you fine?", said her coworker, fascinated by Katherine' odd conduct.

- "Yes, I am OK. I got a new job in a new quiet town, the way I wanted, I have a nice place to live, ...yeah, I feel Ok.

- "I can't see how someone would hunt for a location like this to live in. It's a very calm town. Nothing occurs here! No enjoyment, no entertainment, no excellent shops...if I could, I would go away.

At least I have relatives. I am not alone here. I have my spouse, my kid, mother, father, and my family around. But you have no one here. Don't you feel lonely?".

- "Well, sometimes I do. But I also appreciate it, being alone. I just don't mind".

- "And how do you spend your leisure time?"

- "I clean the apartment, iron the clothes, watch TV, make the weekly shopping, because we don't have much time in the middle of the week, I phone my family occasionally, I try a new dish...", and while thinking of food, Katherine recalled that she should not eat too much, otherwise she would feel bad.

- "The entire time alone! You should at least have a partner, but I have terrible news, you won't get anybody fascinating on this end of the planet," she said. Jane grinned.

- "At least not for now, I'm not looking for a relationship."

"You didn't eat much," I said.

- "I'm content."

- "I should be able to control my eating, but I just can't. I adore pasta! On Sundays, after returning from church, we usually cook a large lunch at my parents' house, consisting entirely of Italian cuisine.

We all get together, chat a lot, eat a lot, sing a lot, and drink a lot. Perhaps you'd like to join us next Sunday ".

I promised my mother to contact her on Sunday afternoon, but I don't know.

- "You may either come with us to the church for the mass and then we can go directly to my mother's house for lunch, or you can come with us to the church and then return home to call your mom in the afternoon.

You must like pasta and be a Catholic, right? "Eugênia smiled broadly and inquired, as if it were apparent that anyone who lived there would enjoy pasta and be a Catholic.

Katherine smiled in response to the colleague and said, "Yes. I appreciate the offer, but I'm sorry we'll have to postpone it until another time since I had intended to use this weekend to arrange some clothing and files at home, which would take up a lot of time.

- "As you want," a dissatisfied Eugênia said.

"This church, you mean the chapel up on the hill where you used to attend mass, no"?

"No, no, there are no masses at that church. It's in the next town, a little larger than that ancient chapel."

"No? How not? I thought there was a mass there every Sunday."

- "There is nothing there; the church has been vacant for a long time. Once, a man attempted to provide some amusement to this deserted town, and he was granted permission to turn it into a disco.

He maintained the main nave as if it were still a church and furnished the side rear chambers with weird furniture, crimson wall coverings, and red carpets, creating an eerie ambiance.

The disco was constantly packed, drawing patrons from other towns as well, but I only went once to get a feel for it and never returned.

Some rumors began to circulate that the disco was impolite, a hub for the trade of illegal narcotics, and even a promiscuous, decadent location where individuals readily misbehaved.

After this incident, that condemned chapel was forgotten about once again. Apparently, a short circuit caused the chapel to catch fire, although other individuals claim that it was not an accident ".

Katherine found it difficult to accept what she had just heard so rapidly.

"And whatever became of the guy who created this disco?"

No one is sure, but I believe he departed the town.

"But what about the priest over there," you ask.

There isn't a priest there, so who is that, I ask.

"Priest Arthur, I saw him there once."

"Priest Arthur? I don't know a priest in our parish by that name, and I'm certain there isn't a priest in that deserted chapel," a parishioner said.

Katherine experienced static! Exactly where is her covert chastity belt? She pondered. And the customs she followed? Can it be possible that a common mad guy lied to me so much and exploited me the whole time given the humiliation she endured and the glass with her pubic hairs at the altar? She questioned. The key, what about it? If this guy vanishes without a trace, how can I get rid of this belt? While the server brought the bill to the table, Katherine worriedly bowed her head.

Are you OK? You seemed abruptly depressed. Did I say anything incorrectly?

"No, not at all. Let's get back to the workplace. What exactly do I do there?"

Katherine made the decision to leave her job and return to the church to look into it further. She really hoped that the priest would be there this time and that her colleague was mistaken.

The chapel's entrance was once again open. No one was present when Katherine entered. No one picked up when she phoned using the priest's name. Another surprise awaited her as she entered the punishment chamber, which by this point she was well familiar with.

There were no longer any portraits, crosses on the walls, ribbons hanging from the ceiling, toilet paper on the seat, glasses, wine or water bottles, candlesticks, or candles anywhere in the room. It had the precise appearance of an ancient, abandoned chamber. She made the decision to inspect the next room, something she had not done previously.

Except for a few charred red wallpaper remnants at the wall and a few broken electrical lines, there was nothing there. Her colleague didn't appear to be in error. Katherine felt astonished.

She thought while leaning against the dusted wall with her lips wide. Katherine came to the conclusion that either priest Arthur was one of those horny spirits who wanted to take advantage of her, or she had been severely duped by a forger. She feared, "I have to obtain the key to this belt."

He told me to return to the chapel on the following Sunday. "He is definitely a totally crazy man, but I must get this key. He will probably decorate that room again for me on Sunday and he shouldn't know that I already know that he is not a priest or who knows, what a crazy man like him is able to do? This is crazy! I will come back on Sunday," Katherine decided incredulously.

Part 5: The Permanence Of The Spirits

Despite the lie, Katherine improved her appearance for the Sunday meeting with Arthur. She was really unsure of whether she exerted so much effort because she was attracted to the guy or because she was afraid of the circumstance.

She thought about all the work dad was doing to get the chapel ready for these rites while she was driving there. He obviously enjoyed their time together, she reasoned.

Katherine parked the vehicle, made her way to the large front chapel entrance, halted for a little while in front of it, pushed her skirt down, and made an attempt to enter with confidence while seeming as if she knew nothing.

Her strategy was to get the key without engaging in another sexual rite. She would tell Arthur what she had learned about that church once she obtained the key, and she would undoubtedly dispute it with him. She walked in.

Since she did not see Arthur on the bench, he was presumably inside already. Surprisingly, as she approached the punishment chamber, it was still vacant.

She briefly felt anxious. Except for a white object on the desk, there was nothing there. It was a letterhead with her name. She opened right away, cautiously interested. The key and a letter were both present.

Once she had the key, she was much relieved and unlocked her chastity belt right away. When she realized she was no longer bound by that restriction, she grinned. She put the letter on the desk after taking off the belt and reading it:

"Hello Katherine

From the top of my sacred position, I absolve you from your sins. I prayed a lot for you and for the spirits souls. You can be free now and sleep well. I do not believe you will be pestered by bad spirits any longer. I am so sorry; I am not there today to help you. I was transferred suddenly to another parish and had to leave immediately. I should have written down your address or telephone number.

I'm wishing you the best.

Father Arthur"

Katherine became upset, indignant, annoyed, sad, angry once again, and outraged. She departed after taking the belt with her as a memento.

She reasoned that even if the church was deserted, she could not leave that item there. Katherine drove back to her house furious with both Arthur and herself for being so foolish and allowing herself to be so cruelly mistreated.

She was now simply hostile toward him. She pondered what she would do with herself, her better-dressed self, and her intense anger the rest of the Sunday. Katherine struggled to stop having negative thoughts for the remainder of the day.

Katherine could not conceal her grumpiness when she came to work each day as the week dragged on. After a few days of being home alone, she lost control and broke down in tears.

She sobbed for 15 minutes until she stopped, feeling as if it made no sense to mourn for a guy she didn't even know, who had lied to her repeatedly and abused her so much. She said to herself, "But I have no one anymore, and I miss that bastard!"

Eugênia felt compelled to inquire about Katherine' wellbeing.

Katherine said, "Yes, everything is good," her cheeks puffy from sobbing.

"I apologize if I am being too inquisitive, but it seems that you have been weeping. I'm concerned about you. You don't look so cheerful these days."

Katherine lied, saying, "That's okay. It's just that I miss my family."

- "Oh, I can understand. You showed a great deal of emotional independence, but when it comes to family, I believe we are all the same. We can't break the tight ties for so long. Why don't you join my family this Sunday for the lunch that you declined the previous time?" After giving it some thought, Katherine responded.

"Okay, I'll go this time."

"Great! My family will lift your spirits, I know they always are," she said.

"Thanks, Eugênia,"

You're welcome; see, here's my address; I'll meet you there at 12:30, all right?; and if you need help finding the place, just give me a call.

"Thank you," Katherine said with a grin to her coworker.

Another Sunday had arrived, and as Katherine prepared for the Eugênia family meal, she reflected on how wonderful Sundays were typically since it was when she first met priest Arthur. Or simply

Arthur, she thought, correcting the way she had spoken to him.

The large family of Eugenia welcomed Katherine with open arms. All of them were kind, made an effort to include her in the group's harmony, and struck up a conversation with her on their own to get to know her better. Despite being stunned by their warmth, Katherine was still very distressed. Nothing in the area could make her laugh out loud involuntarily and honestly.

The following week did not alter much. Katherine attempted to resurrect her own, often harmful, sexual fantasies during the course of the weekend when she was home alone.

When she felt her own touch, she quickly remembered the chastity belt. I should be thrilled with the fact that I no longer have it and can feel my whole body, but I'm not, she moaned. Nothing could pull her attention away from Arthur.

She instantly felt that she despised him, mostly because she had grown to rely inexplicably on him over a short period of time. She swore at him aloud before closing her eyes.

On the open couch bed she had in her living room, Katherine fell asleep. She began dreaming, and it was a pleasant dream. She unwinded. Eroticism, religion, and mysticism were all present in her dream.

In her dream, strange masculine forms with odd masks appeared. When a voice murmured in her ear, she wasn't afraid—instead, she was really enjoying herself. The cafe, the cafe, the cafe. She was startled when she awoke and immediately sat down to attempt to understand what had happened.

She got to her feet, walked to the kitchen to get some water, made herself a snack, and attempted to recall her dream. After a long time, she finally smiled naturally as she thought about Arthur. Katherine bemoaned once more, "I've never had such nasty and wonderful sex in my life as I did with this bogus priest.

She made the decision to drink coffee in addition to the sandwich. She made the coffee while still feeling half asleep while holding the plate with the sandwich on it with her left hand.

She sensed a presence next to her and a voice in her ear as soon as she raised the saucer. She became frightened, stumbled, and rejected the cup of coffee.

The ghosts appear to want me to go to the café, she remarked aloud, prompting her to grab a piece of paper to wipe the liquid away and a moist towel to clean the coffee.

On Mondays, the Café Sechxpresso was closed, which is when Katherine first met Arthur. But on Tuesday, Katherine went there for lunch. She wasn't sure why she went there this time, but she had a strong intuition that she should.

Katherine sat down at a desk. She placed an order before the waiter arrived. She recalled how Arthur had approached her at that location. She used to be afraid of the ghosts, but for some reason she had forgotten about it now.

She took a thoughtful glance around. The Café was not very crowded at the time. The neighboring customer exited the café while standing up and leaving the local newspaper on the table two tables away. Katherine spoke to the waiter as he brought her drinks.

It seems that your other customer left his newspaper there, so thank you.

Oh no, it's not his. We have a local tabloid here that we usually purchase and have available for customers to read as they enjoy their coffee. Would you want to read it and have some fun with it?

"Why not? "

The server finished the conversation and handed Katherine the tabloid. Katherine gently flipped the pages as she waited for her dinner, stopping at one with an almost half-page illustration of an odd location with a crowd of happy people drinking in it and a large cross in the distance.

She became interested and began reading the article about the new pub that had just opened in a nearby town that was just 15 kilometers away. Due to its play with religious artifacts, the bar was raising a little bit of controversy in the community.

A large cross, chapel pews, chalices, strange paintings of the devil on the walls, and even an altar could be found there.

However, the location looked to be a major success among the young people and those not so young who are interested in exploring the local area with the new concept. Catholic devotees of the area are gathering petitions to denounce sacrilege. "The Sinner" is the name of the pub.

"Arthur! I discovered him, thanks to the aid of the spirit voice!" Katherine exclaimed loudly and thoughtfully.

When the waiter returned and handed her order, she was unable to conceal her immediate smile. Katherine quickly regained the tremendous vitality she had been missing throughout the previous days.

She began to make plans for how she would curse in Arthur's face as she drove to this location.

She saw herself doing these rituals most likely with every second lady who walked into his bar. She hated him even more because she knew she wasn't the only victim. She wanted to exact some kind of retaliation on him or at the least, demonstrate his extreme evil.

When the weekend arrived, Katherine made the decision to go to the town where the bar "The Sinner" was situated straight away on Saturday.

She prepared herself for a potential encounter with Arthur all morning until 14:00, at which point she left her house. Since "The Sinner" wouldn't start until 20:00, Katherine would have plenty of time to tour the nearby town and find a place to stay the night.

She didn't want to drive home in the dark. It's also possible that she might need to consume a little more alcohol in order to motivate herself for a difficult conversation with Arthur.

Katherine walked to a nearby food shop and purchased her a bottle of red wine after booking a hotel for the night. She made the decision to freshen up her makeup while sipping wine at 19:00 in the evening. Making the appropriate makeup at that time seemed more challenging in some way. She created andrew eyeliner three times.

By the time 20:30 rolled around, Katherine was still in her room. It was nearly 21:00 when she finally departed after applying a little extra perfume behind the ears. I think I'm too anxious; I didn't plan to be here this late, she reasoned.

Oops! This picture does not adhere to our content standards. Please delete it or post an alternative picture if you want to continue publishing.

To get into "The Sinner," there was a line. The ancient, large home had several lights in front of it, and the windows had something like a mosaic with vibrant paintings that recalled church windows. There was a large sign that said "The Sinner" at the top of the façade.

Katherine entered and made an effort to comprehend her surroundings in the midst of the throng. The tabloid described church pews as seating for some of the long, old-fashioned tables that were distributed around the rooms.

The large black cross in the center of the main chamber created a particularly false religious ambiance. A massive black chandelier hanging from the ceiling and an altar with two urns in front of the cross completed the ornate interior design of the area.

The rooms off to the side featured crimson and gold decor that matched what Katherine observed in the church. There was a large bar in one of the rooms of the home. The beverages were served in unique cups that resembled a chalice.

The apartments' ceilings were decorated with religious symbols. Pictures of religious and sensual rituals were all around the home. Katherine followed them and halted her steps just in front of the devil's painting, which she was previously aware of from the church.

She spent more than a minute gazing at the picture as she thought back on the bizarre experience she had with the liar. She quickly lost her cool and experienced the well-known sense of being grossly mistreated. I detest this crapula, she thought one again.

She turned to face the photo and saw Arthur, who was wearing a priest's black tunic with a white collar, standing just behind her, looking at her intently and closely since the room was packed. She reasoned that his priestly attire was undoubtedly a marketing ploy for his company.

It's nice to see Katherine again. Katherine quavered.

"Well.. I don't know yet whether I can say the same," she said coldly, her eyes locked on his somber expression. Arthur could sense her resentment right away.

He confidently said, "Come, let me buy you a drink," while grasping her arm and leading her through the crowd to the bar. He asked for two wine glasses, which came in gold chalices.

- He wished her "Cheers". She did communicate.

Katherine said sternly, "The only thing that can be said about you is that you are really creative.

He said, "That is not entirely accurate in your statement. "I did everything I could to aid you; I freed you from the belt and the evil spirits, and it appears I accomplished something good, since otherwise I think you wouldn't be here right now."

Cynically defending himself, Arthur. I hope you've received the letter, or are you still wearing the chastity belt, since I had to leave right away as I said in the letter.

I've read the letter, and it seems that the spirit next to me is the worst one—"No, I'm not," the speaker said.

You are an amazing lady, and I did not want those evil spirits to make you even more afraid than you were when we met. - Arthur distrusted his own words, "I see you are still angry with me; I am very sorry. "How did you find me here?" I asked.

"The good spirits assisted me, or should I think that, it is a trap of the evil ones,"

What do you mean when you say they assisted you?

When I arrived at the Sechxpresso Café, I saw a tabloid on a table and read in it that this bar with the name "The Sinner" had opened. It was easy to draw the conclusion that only you could be responsible because they had been whispering in my ears to go there.

"Very clever, I'm glad the spirits sent you here; obviously, they approve of our ceremonies, and I presume you don't have any more issues with them," said the priest.

Katherine was unable to hear him because of the loud music and crowd noise.

What exactly did you say?

To rephrase the message, Arthur drew nearer to her ear. Katherine had enough reason to understand that she would be unable to stop him. She gave him a sideways grin before kissing him. Arthur exchanged emails.

"Katherine, I have to say, you are a real sinner, and I appreciate the fact that you don't conceal it," the person said.

"No, I'm not; I'm a victim," I said.

"So, why did you come here?"

Katherine lied, saying, "Well, the evil spirits are bothering me again. It is terrible. Since you left, I could hardly sleep. They seem to be everywhere. I felt one touching my leg one of these nights, when I was almost asleep, and two days ago I felt a pinch on my nipple. You are the only one I could talk about it with.

- "And"?

"And I figured maybe you might assist me,"

You're correct, your situation is special and serious, and I'm the only one who can assist you, Arthur said while giving her another kiss. "I think we cannot disregard the seriousness of the matter. We must go through with the rituals until the spirits are happy. And it appears that it will not happen so fast. Why don't we meet tomorrow at the chapel?"

"I'm afraid you're correct. Tomorrow," perhaps?

"Yes, tomorrow. Sunday once again."

- "At 17:00"?

"The same time,"

Both of them felt relieved as they kissed. Before leaving the pub, Katherine shared one more wine glass with Arthur. He handed her his confidential business card, which read as follows:

In "The Sinner"

Giovanni Carbone

Marketing Director

He approached the bartender for a pen, snatched the card out of her hands, and overstruck "Your Priest" where the term "Marketing Manager" should have been.

In "The Sinner"

Giovanni Carbone

Marketing Director's Priest

He gave Katherine another kiss as she grinned.

Katherine remarked, "I must go now or tomorrow I will be too exhausted for the ceremony."

"I understand. I have a job too. This isn't really my favorite position, but we need to all live, or else I'd rather be simply your priest," he said.

Arthur, good night.

"You mean, 'Good night Priest Arthur,'" I asked. Katherine made an effort not to grin.

"Please pardon me, Sir. Good night, Father Arthur." She left content.

The next morning, Katherine drove back home, had a thorough shower, and quickly put on as much makeup as she could. She departed for the church at 16:45 and arrived on time. Her vehicle was parked.

There were no people or other cars in the area. Where might Arthur's automobile be, she pondered. She paused for a moment. Possibly cheating her once again, he chose not to show up.

She nervously got out of the vehicle and made her way to the chapel's main entrance. She paused for a few while in front of the door, pulled her skirt down, and took a big breath.

Her hair was messed up by a sudden, strong breeze. "Enter Katherine!" was murmured in her ear as she attempted to mend them with her fingertips. She responded, turning her head swiftly to the side, getting goosebumps, and walking in, dreading fresh annoyance. On a seat in front of the chapel, next to the altar, Arthur was there.

"Good night, Katherine."

Katherine grinned and said, "Good evening, Priest Arthur."

The End